A Gift from Little Bear

There once was a
little bear who lived
in the woods with
his family.

Their forest
was very old,
thick and wild.

There were plenty of sweet berries and
juicy burdock leaves to eat.

Little Bear loved exploring the forest with his sister.
They tumbled and played under the giant trees.

His mother had warned him not to leave the forest.

"Beware," she said, "there is a campground on the edge of the woods."

"What is a campground?" Little Bear asked.

"That is where the humans stay. And they can be unsafe for bears."

Little Bear decided to stay away from the humans.

One day he was playing on the far edge of the forest and heard new voices. It seemed that someone was playing and having a lot of fun!

Little Bear
became curious.

He remembered the warning his mother had given him, but was intrigued by the noise and moved closer. "I will only take a look from the bushes," Little Bear decided.

He crept up the narrow path and hid in the tall grass.

Little Bear saw human cubs with no fur running around a bright colored den, laughing and calling to each other. The Little Bear thought, "They don't look unsafe, they don't have claws or big teeth!"

The human mother was setting food on the table. Their food looked colorful and smelled pleasant. Little Bear had never seen such food. It came from bright colored noisy bags.

Their mother
called them
to eat, and

the kids
dove in and
munched
with delight.

Little Bear inched forward to get a closer look when he suddenly stepped on a branch, which made a loud CRACK!

At once all three humans turned and saw him.
Little Bear froze.

The children were delighted to see the cute little bear
staring at them. "Can we feed him, Mommy?" they asked.

"Sure," the human mother said. "Poor little baby bear is probably hungry. Let's feed him." And she slowly placed a sandwich on the grass near the bear.

Little Bear suddenly felt very hungry. He carefully came out of the bushes toward the food. The sandwich smelled yummy so he ate it without hesitation.

From deep in the forest, Little Bear heard his mother calling his name. She must be looking for him.

He quickly loped back into the forest. On the way home
Little Bear started to feel sick to his stomach.

He came to his mother and said, "Mommy, I have a tummy ache."

His mother hugged him and kissed his black nose. "What happened?"

"I went to the human meadow and they were so nice to me. They were not unsafe! They gave me their human food."

"Little Bear, human food is not for bears. Bears eat rasp-bear-ies, straw-bear-ies, black bear-ies and blue-bear-ies. And other foods that have the word bear in them, including tu-bears, beary-beary green leaves, and unbearably delicious honey."

"Is bear food good
    for humans?"

"Bear food is good
    for everybody."

That night, Little Bear was thinking so much
he had a hard time falling asleep.

The next morning he woke up at dawn.
Little Bear had an idea.

He found a large burdock leaf
and filled it with the sweetest
wild bear-ies he could find.

Little Bear carried it to the
human meadow.

When the humans saw him, they offered him another sandwich.

Little Bear shook his head, and gently placed his gift on their table.

The berries looked so colorful and juicy!
With great joy the children ate the tasty berries.

Little Bear left them to their eating and
ran back home. This time he felt happy and safe.

ISBN 978-0-9704819-4-8

Library of Congress Control Number: 2011903669

Printed in Canada